THE GOLDEN ARMOUR

ZEPHA
THE MONSTER SQUID

With special thanks to Cherith Baldry

To Rachel Leyshon

www.beastquest.co.uk

ORCHARD BOOKS
338 Euston Road, London NW1 3BH
Orchard Books Australia
Level 17/207 Kent St, Sydney, NSW 2000

A Paperback Original
First published in Great Britain in 2008

Beast Quest is a registered trademark of Working Partners Limited
Series created by Working Partners Limited, London

Text © Working Partners Limited 2008
Cover illustration © David Wyatt 2008
Inside illustrations by Steve Sims © Orchard Books 2008

A CIP catalogue record for this book is available
from the British Library.

ISBN 978 1 84616 988 5

10

Printed and bound in China by Imago

Orchard Books is a division of Hachette Children's Books,
an Hachette UK company.

www.hachette.co.uk

ZEPHA
THE MONSTER
SQUID

BY ADAM BLADE

ORCHARD BOOKS

Did you think it was over?

Did you think I would accept defeat, and disappear?

No! That can never be. I am Malvel, the Dark Wizard who strikes fear into the hearts of the people of Avantia. I still have much more to show this kingdom, and one boy in particular – Tom.

The young hero liberated the six Beasts of Avantia from my curse. But his fight is far from over. Let us see how he fares with a new Quest, one that will surely crush him and his companion, Elenna.

Avantia's Beasts had good hearts that I corrupted for my own wicked purpose. Now, thanks to Tom, they are free to protect the kingdom once more. But I have created six new supreme Beasts whose hearts are evil and so cannot be set free: monster squid, giant monkey, stone charmer, snake man, king of spiders and three-headed lion. Each Beast guards a piece of the most precious relic of Avantia, which I have stolen: the suit of golden armour that gives magical strengths to its rightful owner. I will stop at nothing to prevent Tom collecting the complete suit and defeating me again. This time he will not win!

Malvel

PROLOGUE

King Hugo's master of arms paused
at the foot of the stairs. He smiled to
hear the faint noise of music and
laughter from the Great Hall above.

"Thank goodness," he thought.
"Malvel the Dark Wizard has been
defeated. Avantia is safe again."

He walked down the stone passage
and stopped outside a heavy padded
door, studded with brass nails. He
pulled a slender golden key from his
pocket and held it up. It shone in

a ray of light that reached down from an air vent and pierced the gloom of the palace cellars.

The key turned smoothly when he fitted it into the lock. He pushed the door open and stepped into the arms room, closing the door behind him and locking it. As he did so, a ferret poked its head out of his pocket and peered up at him with bright, curious eyes.

"There we are," the master of arms murmured, stroking the ferret's cream-coloured fur. "Now no one can get in or out."

The room was so small that if the man stretched out his arms, his fingers brushed the walls on either side. Torches blazed in iron holders, casting dancing shadows on the rough stone walls.

In the centre of the room stood a suit of golden armour on a wooden stand. The helmet was dramatically moulded into the shape of an eagle's head; the visor was a sharp beak and the rest of the helmet was engraved with feather-like patterns. The tunic of golden chainmail was covered with a fine breastplate that shone in the torchlight. Glittering leg armour, gauntlets and sabatons – armoured boots – completed the suit.

The master walked slowly around it, examining the armour with a small grunt of satisfaction. He pulled out a handkerchief to rub a speck of dust from the gleaming breastplate.

"I've looked after this armour for twenty years," he said. "When I first set eyes on it, it took my breath away. And do you know what?" He tickled the ferret's ear. "It still does."

The ferret let out a squeak.

"It's the most precious relic in all

Avantia. We've got to keep every bit of it shining as brightly as the day it was made," he went on. "Its rightful owner could return at any moment." He passed the handkerchief over the smooth curve of the helmet. "We must be ready." He bent down to polish the golden feet of the armour.

Suddenly the ferret let out a squeal of alarm. Wriggling out of its master's pocket, it dived for a crack in the wall and disappeared.

"Here!" the man cried. "What's the matter with you?" He put his head on the floor and tried to peer into the crack, but the dancing shadows cast by the torches made it difficult to see. "Where are you? Come back, you silly creature! There's nothing to be afraid of."

But as he spoke, the shadows began to leap, faster and faster, and were soon whirling across the walls and floor. He glanced at the torches, but the bright flames burnt steadily. What could be making the shadows swoop like this?

Then something brushed the man's cheek. He spun round at the velvety touch and stared wildly around the room. "These aren't shadows," he said out loud. "They're bats!"

Suddenly the air was full of black wings. Tiny claws scratched at his face and hands, and tangled in his hair.

"No!" He let out a choking cry and beat desperately at the air, trying to drive the creatures back. But the swarming bats kept coming. He stared in horror at their fierce faces and sharp teeth. Their little eyes glittered cruelly.

Terrified, the master of arms backed towards the door, as more

bats squeezed themselves out of
cracks in the wall and launched
themselves into the air. He felt as if
he couldn't breathe.

Soon the suit of golden armour was covered with bats. They hung all over it, clinging with their hooked claws. Gasping in horror, the master of arms started forward, but his knees gave way and he collapsed to the floor. Still he kept on struggling, trying with all his might to drag himself towards the precious armour.

"Stop!" he gasped. "Help! Please, somebody, help!"

But it was too late. Bats covered the man's head and back, wrenching his hair and suffocating him with their wings. He felt as if every last scrap of air was being pressed out of his lungs, and stared in disbelief as the golden armour rose slowly into the air, lifted by the evil swarm of bats. Only the wooden stand was left.

Then darkness flooded over him.

CHAPTER ONE

GONE!

Tom stood next to a pillar in the
Great Hall of King Hugo's palace, and
watched the dancing. He was elated
to see all the king's subjects
celebrating the end of his Quest.
Their silk and satin robes shone as
they whirled in the afternoon sun.

King Hugo watched from the
High Table with a contented smile. Tom
knew the king was happy that the six

Beasts of Avantia had been released from the evil spell of the Dark Wizard, Malvel. Ferno the fire dragon, Sepron the sea serpent, Arcta the mountain giant, Tagus the horse-man, Nanook the snow monster and Epos the flame bird were now protecting Avantia instead of destroying it. The kingdom could begin to recover.

But Tom couldn't join in the celebrations. Something had been nagging at him ever since that final meeting with Malvel on the mountainside in the far east of the kingdom. He told himself over and over again that Malvel had fallen into the volcano and perished in its raging fires.

But he couldn't forget what Malvel had screamed at him just before he disappeared: "This is not the end, Tom! We shall meet again!"

Tom had a horrible feeling that he hadn't seen the last of his enemy. Then he remembered the hooded figure he had spotted in the cheering crowd when he returned from freeing Epos, the last of the cursed Beasts. If the Dark Wizard had indeed survived, how would he take revenge for his defeat?

Tom shuddered. He wished his father, Taladon the Swift, were here. He had been a knight and had undertaken a Beast Quest of his own. Only he could know how Tom felt. But no one had seen Taladon for many years. It was as if he had disappeared into thin air, although Tom felt certain that they would meet again one day.

Tom felt a hand on his shoulder. He turned to see Elenna, the friend who had shared every step of the Quest with him. She was wearing a dress of blue silk, but her short dark hair stuck out untidily, just as when they'd first met.

"What's the matter, Tom?" she asked. "Why are you looking so worried?"

Tom shook his head uneasily. "I'm not sure... I just keep remembering the last thing that Malvel said on the mountain."

"Malvel is finished," Elenna declared. "There's nothing to worry about." Taking Tom's hand, she dragged him onto the dance floor. "I've just been to the stables. Storm is stuffing himself with the best apples, and look – Silver's enjoying himself under the table there."

Tom smiled as he saw the wolf contentedly gnawing on a bone, and was glad to think of his black stallion enjoying a well-deserved rest in the comfortable palace stables.

"Everyone's happy," Elenna went on. "Can't you be happy, too? Let's dance."

"I don't know how to dance," Tom said, laughing despite his worries.

"I'll show you."

To Tom's relief, the music stopped before Elenna could guide him through more than a few steps.

Then he spotted King Hugo's wizard and adviser, Aduro, making his way towards them. They would never have completed the Quest if it hadn't been for the good wizard, who had helped and encouraged them in their most difficult moments. Now he wore a magnificent embroidered robe and carried a polished wooden staff in one hand. Tom bowed, and Elenna dropped into a deep curtsey.

"Are you enjoying yourselves?" Aduro asked.

"Yes, it's wonderful!" Elenna's eyes sparkled.

The wizard smiled. "If you don't mind missing some of the dancing, I've something to show you. Something in the palace cellars."

"Not more danger?" Tom was instantly alert.

Aduro shook his head, smiling, and Tom realised that even the king's adviser thought Malvel had been defeated for good. "No," the wizard replied. "It's a reward for a successful Quest. Avantia owes you a great deal."

Tom and Elenna followed him to a small door at the far end of the hall and down a long flight of steps. Elenna was bouncing with excitement.

At the foot of the steps was a narrow passage. Aduro led them on, then stopped outside a padded door. A single shaft of light shone down from a high air vent and gleamed on the door's brass nails and lock.

"This is strange," the wizard said. "I was expecting to meet the king's master of arms here. He's not the sort of man to be late. I wonder what has happened to him?"

"Maybe he's inside," Elenna suggested.

Aduro turned the door handle, but the door remained shut. "Locked," he muttered. "Maybe—"

He broke off at the sound of a loud groan coming from inside the room.

Tom and Elenna exchanged a glance.

"It sounds as if someone's hurt," said Tom.

Wizard Aduro laid the end of his staff against the lock and commanded, "Open!"

The lock clicked and the door swung open. Inside the room the body of an elderly man sprawled on the floor. A ferret was nosing anxiously at him.

The man tried to get up, but his strength gave way and he slumped down again.

Tom and Elenna ran to his side. He was barely conscious. His skin was pale, his black tunic was torn, and his face and hands were covered with tiny bites and scratches.

Tom helped the old man to sit up.

"Aduro, can you magic a jug of water for him?" Elenna asked. "Quickly!"

But the wizard simply stared at the space in the middle of the room, empty except for a wooden armour stand. He didn't seem to have heard Elenna's anxious plea. He looked stunned.

Tom jumped to his feet. "What's the matter?" he asked.

Aduro turned to him, blinking as if he were just waking up. "Something terrible has happened." His voice was hoarse. "The golden armour. It's gone!"

CHAPTER TWO

A NEW QUEST

"Can you tell us what happened?"
Aduro asked, kneeling beside the
injured man.

The master of arms drew in
a shaky breath. "Bats!" he whispered.
"The whole room was full of bats.
They took the armour." He covered
his face with his hands. "I have failed
the king."

Aduro touched the old man's

shoulder. "No, my friend. Evil has been at work here." Standing up again, he thumped on the floor three times with his staff.

A moment later, Tom heard running footsteps in the passage and two servants appeared in the doorway. Their eyes grew wide with shock as they looked inside.

"Carry the master to his room,"
Wizard Aduro ordered. "Send for
King Hugo's healer. And mind you
say nothing of this to anyone."

The two servants lifted the elderly
man carefully. Elenna scooped up the
ferret and gave it to the master as he
was carried out into the passage.

As soon as the master of arms
and the servants had gone, Tom turned
to the wizard. "This was Malvel's
work! It must have been. He is still
alive after all."

Aduro nodded gravely. "I fear you
are right."

"What armour were you talking
about?" Elenna asked. "Why is it so
important?"

"Tom, the armour was to have
been your reward, for completing the
Quest," Aduro explained. "Once it
belonged to the Master of the Beasts.

It brings magical strengths to its rightful owner."

"But…" Tom was puzzled. "You couldn't give me the armour if it belongs to the Master of the Beasts. I remember you told me that Malvel had imprisoned him long before my Quest began, but why isn't he still wearing it?"

Aduro let out a long sigh. "Many years ago, the Master of the Beasts should have returned to the palace for the New Year feast. Instead, the empty suit of armour appeared in the Great Hall as the nobles were taking their places." The wizard paused, then went on. "Malvel had captured him, then sent the armour to mock King Hugo – and me."

Tom felt as if an icy hand had clutched his heart. He hoped that the Master of the Beasts had not suffered too greatly in the hands of the Dark Wizard.

"However, I felt that all was not lost," Aduro said. "The powers of the armour would still work if the suit was worn by the right person – a true Quester with brave blood running through his veins. I think you are that person, Tom."

For a moment Tom could not speak. He wasn't sure he was worthy to wear the golden armour. But he would give everything to protect Avantia.

The wizard began to pace back and forth impatiently across the small room, his staff clicking on the stone floor. "Malvel must have realised that your successful Quest has made you a danger to him. He would never have imagined that anyone – much less a boy – could lift the spells on all six Beasts. He has stolen the armour to stop you wearing it and gaining its magical powers."

"But it would never fit me." Tom measured himself against the wooden stand that had held the armour. "It must have been made for a tall man."

"The armour will shrink or expand to fit the one who wears it," Aduro explained. "It will know who truly deserves it."

"Then we have to do something!" Elenna's eyes sparkled with indignation. "We can't let Malvel get away with this."

More cautiously, Tom added, "But first we must find out what really happened to the armour."

Aduro halted in his pacing. He raised his staff and swept it in a wide arc. The air glittered in its wake and a picture gradually formed, hovering above them.

Tom and Elenna let out gasps of wonder and fear.

They could see a multitude of flying bats, carrying pieces of the golden armour hooked in their claws. Then the swarm split up. Groups of bats flew off in six different directions, each carrying a part of the armour. The sound of Malvel's mocking laughter grew until it filled the room.

Then the vision faded. When it had quite gone, Aduro let out a weary sigh. "This is worse than I feared. Malvel's bats have scattered the armour around the kingdom." He looked gravely at Tom. "Are you ready for another Quest, so soon after your first? Will you seek out the pieces of armour and bring them back together?"

Tom drew himself up. "Of course I will."

"And what about me?" Elenna asked with a fierce look. "Where Tom goes, I go!"

A relieved smile spread over Aduro's face. "Thank you, Elenna. I know that you too have the courage to succeed. My magic map will show you where to go. I'll fetch it while you change into travelling clothes. Meet me in the stables as soon as you can."

Tom hurried back to his room and changed into a woollen tunic and sturdy boots. He fastened on his scabbard, sheathed his sword and picked up his shield. It bore the six magical tokens from the Beasts he had freed: Ferno's dragon-scale protected him from heat, Sepron's tooth from onrushing water, Arcta's eagle feather from great heights, and Nanook's bell from extreme cold. Tagus's horseshoe fragment gave him extra speed and Epos's golden talon healed wounds.

Surely their combined power would strengthen him now?

Then Tom went down to the stables. As he crossed the courtyard Elenna caught up with him, Silver at her heels.

"I took some food left over from the feast," she said, showing Tom a large bundle wrapped in a white cloth.

"Good thinking," Tom said, smiling. He knew he and Elenna made a great team.

Aduro was waiting in the stables. A groom had already saddled Storm. Elenna stroked the black stallion's nose and fed him one last apple.

"Here is the magic map." The wizard held the familiar parchment scroll out to Tom. "Guard it well. And take care. This time Malvel knows you are a threat to him. His magic is clearly as strong as ever, and now he is angry."

"I'm not afraid of Malvel," Tom said bravely, resting his hand on the hilt of his sword.

Storm snorted, rapping one hoof against the stable floor, and Silver let out a howl of agreement.

Tom climbed into Storm's saddle and Elenna scrambled up behind him.

"Farewell," said Aduro. "And may good luck go with you."

He ordered the guards to open the gates of the palace.

Tom urged Storm into a trot. As they passed through the gates, with Silver bounding alongside, Tom could still hear music and the sounds of celebration ringing out from the palace walls. The rest of Avantia had no idea that Malvel was alive and plotting once more.

Tom was determined that the Dark Wizard would not succeed. He and Elenna would follow this new Quest to the end.

I'm ready, Tom thought. *While there's blood in my veins, I'll do everything I can to protect my home!*

CHAPTER THREE

MALVEL'S WARNING

"I'm glad you're here," Tom told Elenna as they rode away from the palace. "I know we can do this together."

"Silver and Storm will help us, too," Elenna said. "And don't forget the Beasts. They're friendly now, and it's their job to protect Avantia. Maybe we can call on them to help us fight Malvel."

"That's true," said Tom, feeling a swell of determination. With Elenna, their animal friends and the Beasts of Avantia on his side, he knew that it was his destiny to defeat the Dark Wizard.

The road they were following led through fields where cattle grazed peacefully. A few trees grew here and there in the lush grass; the afternoon sun cast long shadows.

Soon they came to a crossroads. Tom brought Storm to a halt and pulled out Wizard Aduro's enchanted map. As he unrolled it a red path began to glow, leading to the coast.

"That's the road we took when we met Sepron the sea serpent," Elenna pointed out, peering over Tom's shoulder.

"Then at least we know the way." Tom felt more cheerful. He rolled up the map, put it back in the saddlebag, and urged Storm on.

They passed through a narrow belt of trees and began to climb a hill. Tom noticed that the sunlight was growing hazy, as though night was falling. A chill wind whispered over him. But the sun still stood well above the horizon, and the sky was blue except for a few puffs of white cloud. Uneasily Tom glanced around. He couldn't see anything except trees and fields.

Then he looked up. High above in the blue sky, black dots were flitting back and forth. Tom remembered the vision Aduro had shown them. "Bats!" he exclaimed.

He felt Elenna lock her arms tightly around his waist. "I thought bats only flew by night," she said.

"Malvel can make his bats fly

anytime," Tom replied grimly.

He reined Storm in, and gripped the hilt of his sword, ready to draw it. The black stallion threw his head up and his harness jingled. Beside the horse, Silver stood stiff-legged, barking angrily at the sky.

The bats flew lower and lower,

until they were swooping around Tom and Elenna. Storm snorted nervously; Tom patted his neck to reassure him. Silver leapt into the air, snapping vainly at the leathery wings.

Tom and Elenna had to duck to avoid the creatures' talons. Tom didn't dare try to outrun them on Storm; the path was steep and rough, and the stallion could easily have been injured. Desperately he drew his sword and slashed at the whirling pack of bats. They fluttered upwards out of range and then clustered together in a rolling ball.

Elenna gasped in astonishment. "What are they doing?"

Slowly the ball took on a different shape. Icy fear rushed through Tom as he recognised the hooded being that had laughed at him so cruelly on that mountainside. It stretched across half the sky, from above Tom's head to the distant horizon.

"Malvel!" he exclaimed.

The Dark Wizard was using the bats to give form to his evil face. Tom could see the gleam of his sunken eyes and the twisted line of his cruel mouth. Mocking laughter poured out and

Malvel's voice boomed around them.

"I hope you enjoyed my surprise. Fools, to think you can defeat me!"

Tom raised his sword. "I know we can defeat you. We'll track down every piece of the armour that you have stolen. Nothing is going to stop us!"

Malvel's laughter echoed again. "Nothing? Not even six new Beasts with evil hearts? Beasts that I have created?"

For a moment Tom was shocked into silence.

Silver let out a miserable whine, and hurled himself into the air again, snapping at Malvel's shape.

"New Beasts!" Elenna exclaimed. "What does he mean?"

Malvel replied. "You'll find out soon enough, when you meet Zepha. Maybe then you'll change your minds and go running home with your tails between your legs."

"Never!" Tom cried defiantly. "You can conjure up whatever Beasts you like, but they won't stop me. I'll never fail Avantia!"

But who – or what – was Zepha? Tom felt a lurch of fear in the pit of his stomach as he thought of the six new Beasts he would have to face.

Then the bats began to scatter. Malvel's face broke up and disappeared, but his jeering laughter echoed around the hills until every last bat had vanished.

Tom sheathed his sword. His stomach was still churning. Elenna looked white and shaken. Storm was sweating and trembling, and Silver's tail was dragging in the dust of the road.

"I think we should make camp," Tom said, trying to keep his voice firm. "We need time to get over that.

And the sun's going down. It'll be dark soon."

Elenna nodded in agreement. They dismounted and Tom led the way to a small clump of woodland not far from the road. There was a pool in the middle of the trees, at the bottom of a rocky hollow. Tom unsaddled Storm while Elenna collected wood and made a fire. They were both glad of the bright flames as the sun set and darkness crept around them.

Elenna unpacked the food she had saved from the feast and handed Tom some bread and cold chicken. "I wonder why Aduro didn't warn us about the new Beasts," she said.

"Perhaps he doesn't know about them," Tom replied. "This is a different Quest. We can't rely on Aduro for everything. This time we're on our own."

Elenna's eyes shone with determination. "We'll manage," she said. "We've got to."

When they had finished eating Tom lay down beside the remains of the fire. He gazed up into the sky. The moon was sailing behind wisps of cloud; there was no sign of any bats.

But now Tom knew that something else was out there. Something more dangerous than

Malvel's vicious bats.

A new set of evil Beasts.

Maybe they were already padding around him, hidden by the night. Tom peered into the shadows, but he couldn't see anything.

It took a long time for sleep to come.

CHAPTER FOUR

DANGER AT SEA

By noon the next day they were drawing near the coast. Tom remembered how they had struggled through the flood waters that Sepron the sea serpent had caused in his rage. Now the land was clear again, with crops growing and people working in the fields, and the houses had been repaired with new wood and thatch. Tom felt proud that he had helped make Avantia prosperous again.

At last the road led Tom and his friends through a patch of thin woodland and out onto the shore.

"Look!" exclaimed Elenna, pointing. "All the fishermen's huts have been rebuilt. And there are lots of new fishing boats."

At first Tom was pleased to see the snug new huts and the brightly painted boats pulled up on the beach, with fishing nets piled high beside them. Then he frowned.

"Shouldn't all those boats be out at sea?" he asked. He exchanged an uncertain glance with Elenna. "What's going on here?"

"There's a smell of dead fish, too," said Elenna, wrinkling her nose.

Tom spotted a wisp of smoke rising from behind some boulders further along the beach. He and Elenna dismounted. Leaving Storm to crop the grass under the trees, they headed for the rocks. As they drew closer they saw a group of people crouched around a driftwood fire. One woman was ladling stew from an iron pot into wooden bowls. All the people looked worried and miserable.

Then Tom recognised a tall boy with red hair and a freckled face. "Calum!" he exclaimed.

The boy looked up, and sprang to his feet. "Tom!" He hugged Tom and then Elenna, before bending down to plunge his hands into the thick fur round Silver's neck. "It's good to see you again."

"It's good to see you, too," Tom said. He would never forget how Calum had helped him when he came to free Sepron the sea serpent from Malvel's evil spell.

"What's going on here?" Elenna asked.

"Yes, why is no one out in the boats?" Tom added.

The men and women round the fire exchanged nervous glances.

"It's too dangerous to go out to sea," Calum explained after a moment's hesitation. "A couple of our people didn't come back yesterday. We found wreckage washed up, but no one knows what happened to the boatmen."

Tom glanced swiftly at Elenna. She was looking as confused as he felt. Sepron was free now, and should have been protecting this part of the kingdom. What had gone wrong?

"Do you know why they disappeared?" he asked Calum.

A man Tom recognised as Calum's father pointed out to sea.

"Whirlpools," he said. "They appeared a few days ago near those rocks. No one knows why. Only a fool would go out there now."

"Or Lindon," another man said with a bitter laugh.

"Who's Lindon?" Tom asked.

"A stubborn fool," the man replied.

"He doesn't know what's good for him," a woman chimed in. "He insisted on going out this morning, trawling for fish, just as he always does. He hasn't returned yet."

"And goodness knows why he went," Calum's father added grumpily. "The pickings are thin enough. Since the whirlpools appeared, all the fish have gone."

"Some of them have been washed up dead," Calum said, pointing to the edge of the water.

Tom could see the gleam of silver

fish lying among the other debris. Silver trotted down to the water's edge and snuffled at one of them. Then he drew back with a disgusted snort.

"Silver! Here, boy." Elenna tickled the wolf's ears as he returned to her. "Be careful where you push your nose."

"These were good fishing waters," the woman went on. "But if the whirlpools stay, we'll have nothing but a few vegetables to live on."

Tom gazed at Calum. The boy's eyes were filled with hope. He was the only one from this village who knew that Tom had freed Sepron from Malvel's curse.

"I think I might know something about this," Tom said softly, so that only Calum could hear. "Wait here."

Beckoning to Elenna, he hurried back to where they had left Storm. He pulled the magic map out of the saddlebag. When he unrolled it, he could see a picture of a golden helmet resting in the sea beside a rocky islet.

"That's exactly where the whirlpools are," said Elenna.

Tom met her anxious gaze. His pulse began to race with a mixture of fear and excitement.

"You heard what Calum said," Elenna went on. "Boats that go out there don't come back."

Tom gazed out across the waves. "I don't have a choice," he said. "This is my Quest. I have to go."

CHAPTER FIVE

LINDON

Tom put the map back into Storm's saddlebag. As he turned to the shore once again, he spotted a fishing boat sailing round a headland towards the beach, its white sail billowing.

"That must be Lindon," he said. "Maybe he'll take us out to the whirlpools in his boat. Come on!"

Tom and Elenna hurried down to

the water's edge, Silver and Storm
trotting behind.

The boat soon reached the beach,
and the fisherman leapt out and
pulled it up beside the other vessels.
He lifted the reed baskets out of the
boat, but Tom could see there were
only a few fish at the bottom.

"Are you Lindon?" Tom asked.

"That's me." The fisherman
dumped the last basket on the beach
and straightened up. He was a tall

young man with shaggy dark hair.
His face was harsh and unfriendly.
"Who wants to know?"

"I do. I need to go out to sea. Will
you take me?"

"I might, if the price is right," Lindon
replied. "Where do you want to go?"

"Over there." Tom pointed out
towards the rocky islet.

Lindon raised his eyebrows. "There
are whirlpools out there. That will
cost extra."

Tom exchanged a glance with Elenna. "I can't afford to pay you," he began, "but—"

"That's all right." Tom realised that Lindon was staring past him at Silver. "You can pay in kind. I'll take that mutt off your hands."

Elenna stepped in front of the wolf. She looked furious at the suggestion that she would hand over her faithful friend. The hair on Silver's spine rose up and he let out a soft growl.

"We can't do that," Tom said firmly. "Isn't there something else you want? Or anything we could do for you?"

Lindon narrowed his eyes. "Why do you want to go out there, anyway?" he asked.

Tom knew he couldn't tell anyone about his Quest. The first time had been bad enough, with the good Beasts of Avantia under terrible curses.

But now that Malvel had unleashed his own evil Beasts on the kingdom it was even more vital to keep the Quest a secret. The people of Avantia would panic if they knew what the Dark Wizard was up to. "I have something important to do," he said.

Lindon let out a bark of rough laughter. "Something important? A boy like you? You'll have to tell me more than that if you want my help."

Tom saw that Elenna was red with anger on his behalf. He had to act quickly before she said something they would both regret.

He remembered then how the people of the village had suggested Lindon liked to take risks. Maybe he would help if he thought that Tom was looking for danger.

"I want to see if I can survive diving into a whirlpool," Tom said, puffing out his chest. "And I've also heard all your fish have died. Maybe I can discover what's causing it."

Lindon stared at him for a moment in astonishment. Then he shook his head and laughed. "Well, you're a mad one and no mistake," he said and paused, a sly look passing over his face. "If you don't come back, I'll have your fine-looking horse." He nodded to Storm, who pawed the ground anxiously. "If you do make it, I'll just shake you by the hand and wish you well." He sighed. "Who knows? Maybe you can find out what is killing our fish. We'll all starve if it continues."

Tom stroked Storm's neck. "Don't worry, boy, I'll be back," he said reassuringly, but he couldn't ignore the swelling fear in his stomach.

Tom had faced danger before.

But now he had to defeat Zepha and find the golden helmet. Because if he didn't he would lose his horse, if not his life. Not to mention leaving the golden armour in Malvel's evil grasp.

CHAPTER SIX

OUT TO SEA

"I'm coming with you," Elenna said, as Lindon made the boat ready.

"No," Tom told her. "Defeating Zepha and finding the helmet is my task. I need you to stay here and look after Silver and Storm."

Elenna bit her lip, then nodded. Tom unfastened his scabbard and handed it to her.

"You might need this," he said.

"And my shield is tied to Storm's saddle. The people here are desperate; they could be dangerous. And you never know what Malvel might do."

Elenna hesitated. "But won't you need your sword and shield?" she asked.

Tom knew he would be vulnerable without them – but there was no way he was leaving Elenna alone and unarmed. He'd just have to rely on his wits. He took Elenna's hand and wrapped her fingers round the hilt of the sword. "I'll be fine," he told her.

"I'll stay with Calum and his father," she said. "I've nothing to fear from them. But Tom, be careful. Remember what Malvel said about Zepha."

Cold fear gripped Tom again. He didn't even know what Zepha was. How could he prepare to fight an evil Beast when he had no idea what it looked like?

"Are you coming or not?" Lindon's harsh voice interrupted his thoughts.

"I'm coming," said Tom, pushing down his apprehension.

Elenna grasped his hand. "Good luck," she said.

Silver added an encouraging bark and Storm whinnied.

"Don't worry. I'll be back soon," Tom promised.

He helped Lindon push the boat back into the water and scrambled over the side. Lindon raised the sail and soon the boat was scudding over the waves again. Tom looked back at the shore where Elenna, Silver and Storm stood. Already they seemed very small and distant.

The sky was covered with thick, grey cloud. As Lindon steered the boat out to sea, the wind grew even stronger. The water became choppy and the boat pitched up and down on the waves.

Tom gripped the side and stared down into the sea. He thought he could make out the movement of some dark shape far beneath the surface. Suddenly the water began to churn angrily and Tom gasped as he realised that the boat was swirling around in a huge circle. A whirlpool was starting up – and he and Lindon were at the centre of it!

Lindon laughed. "Getting scared?" he taunted. "Do you want to change your mind?"

"No!" Tom was determined not to let Lindon see he was afraid. "This is what I've come for."

Lindon grunted and deftly steered the boat out of the whirlpool. Tom could tell he was a skilful sailor. Even so, the boat rocked dangerously and water slopped over the side, soaking Tom. Lindon guided the boat to the edge of the churning water. "I'll wait for you here," he said. "Mind you're not too long! Otherwise I'll be heading back to collect your horse."

Tom climbed onto the side of the
boat. The water was circling faster
than ever, opening up a cone-shaped
passage into the depths of the sea.
Tom's heart thumped in terror, but
he knew he couldn't turn back. He
remembered how he had dived into

the sea to meet Sepron, and had emerged victorious.

"I have to do this," Tom muttered. "For the golden armour. And to defeat Malvel."

Tom took in a lungful of air, and closed his mouth tightly. Then he dived down into the sea.

CHAPTER SEVEN

INTO THE WHIRLPOOL

At once the whirlpool sucked Tom
down into the depths of the ocean.
The force of the water dragged at his
clothes and wrenched his arms and
legs. Tom felt as if he were being
torn apart.

Swirling water was all around him.
Caught up in the powerful current,
Tom spun round and round. He

fought not to lose his bearings, but soon he couldn't tell whether he was facing the surface of the sea or down towards the ocean bed.

"I'm going to drown!" he thought frantically. Was this the end of his new Quest already?

Then pain stabbed through him as his flailing arm struck something hard. Instinctively he grabbed at it and found he was clinging to a spur of rock that thrust upwards from the ocean bed. Working his way along it, he managed to drag himself out of the force of the whirlpool and calm his panic.

Looking around, he saw the spires and hollows of a coral bed stretching into the distance. Then a dull gleam of gold caught his eye. On one spike of rock rested the golden helmet.

Tom had never seen a helmet like it before. It was shaped like an

eagle's head; the visor was moulded
in the form of a hooked beak, and
the golden surface was patterned to
look like feathers.

Tom was amazed. He couldn't believe how easy this was! He would just collect the helmet, then swim back up to the boat.

Kicking away from the rock, Tom swam towards the golden gleam. But as he reached for the helmet, he spotted movement just beyond. A dark shadow was rising up from behind the rock. It was so huge that it took Tom a moment to realise it was a head, with staring, bulging eyes and a mouth like a gaping beak. Seconds later the body followed, with a mass of giant tentacles. Tom could see through the creature's skin, to where three red hearts were pumping.

Zepha was a giant squid! More than that – a monster squid!

This was the Beast threatening the villagers with starvation by driving all the fish away. Panic froze him. How could he battle such a vast creature?

Its eyes alone were as big as he was and the beak could swallow him up in one gulp.

Before Tom could make a dive for the helmet, the squid hurtled out of its shelter in the coral, its snaking tentacles reaching for Tom.

Tom felt his lungs start to hurt with the effort of holding his breath. As he pushed himself through the water,

away from the grasping tentacles,
he let a few precious bubbles of
air escape from his mouth.

Now he was deep below the surface
with no air, and the monster squid
was between him and the helmet.

What could he do now? And more
to the point: how was he going to get
out of this alive?

CHAPTER EIGHT

UNEXPECTED HELP

Kicking out strongly, Tom tried to swim for the surface while he still had breath in his lungs. At every moment he expected one of Zepha's tentacles to fasten round his ankles, dragging him back into the depths.

Tom's head burst through the surface of the sea; he coughed up water and took in great gulps of air. Blinking to clear his eyes, he spotted Lindon's boat rocking on the waves a few yards away, and swam carefully around the whirlpool towards it. When he reached the boat, Lindon leant over the side to help him on board.

"I reckoned I'd seen the last of you," said Lindon. There was a grudging respect in his tone of voice. He grasped Tom's hand and shook it firmly. "I reckon you can keep your horse after that." He looked at Tom curiously. "What did you see down there?"

"You have to take me back!" Tom gasped. "I need to pick up Elenna."

Lindon saw the determination in his face and nodded. Quickly he hauled on the ropes and soon the boat was plunging back towards the beach.

Elenna was waiting for Tom at the water's edge, holding his sword and shield. She flung them down and hugged Tom as he leapt ashore.

Silver bounded around him excitedly, letting out a howl of welcome.

"You're safe!" Elenna exclaimed. "But where's the helmet?"

"At the bottom of the sea," Tom replied. "Guarded by a giant squid."

"Zepha is a squid?"

"Yes. Elenna – he's huge. A monster." Hesitatingly he added, "I'm not sure I can defeat it."

"Yes, you can." Elenna's voice was encouraging. "Or we can do it together."

Tom was warmed by his friend's courage and loyalty. "I was hoping you'd say that," he said.

He turned back to Lindon, to see the fisherman already heading away, towards the people still huddled around the fire. He was carrying the basket of fish he had caught earlier.

"Hey!" Tom called out. "I need you

to take me out there again."

"I've had my share of risk for today," Lindon said. He shook his head regretfully. "I'm not going back out again. Sorry." He strode off towards the fire.

Elenna and Tom looked at each other. They both knew that Elenna was skilful at handling a boat.

"Do you think we should take it?" Elenna whispered.

"We had to do that last time, when we freed Sepron the sea serpent," Tom replied. "It's for the good of the people here. We have no choice."

When they were sure that no one was looking, Tom fastened on his scabbard and put his shield into the boat. Then he and Elenna climbed in. Silver watched them, letting out a mournful whine.

"All right, you can come, too,"

said Elenna. The wolf's ears went up and he took a flying leap into the boat, which rocked from side to side.

"Storm will be fine," Elenna added. "Calum is looking after him."

Tom's fear returned as Elenna guided the boat out to sea. He imagined one of Zepha's giant tentacles lashing out of the water and pulling the boat down into the depths. All three of them would drown.

"Are you ready for this? It's very dangerous..." he began. Had he made a mistake coming back for his friend?

"We wanted to come, didn't we, Silver?" Elenna said calmly.

Silver gave a yelp of agreement.

"But you haven't seen Zepha. He's terrifying."

Tom almost asked Elenna to turn back. But then he saw a blue glow forming in the air just ahead of the boat. Inside it, Aduro appeared. Tom could still see the tossing waves through his robes. The wizard had sent an illusion of himself, just as he had many times before.

"Don't give up hope, Tom," he said with a smile. "Have you forgotten the help you have with you?"

"What do you mean?" Tom asked.

"When you freed Sepron you were given one of his teeth, which you fixed into your shield," Aduro reminded him.

"Of course!" Tom had forgotten.

Aduro went on. "If you rub the tooth, Sepron himself will come to help. But remember: as a good Beast of Avantia, he can only attack Zepha in order to protect you." The wizard's form began to fade. "Good luck!" he called out before he disappeared altogether.

Tom grabbed his shield and polished Sepron's tooth hard with the sleeve of his tunic.

At first nothing happened. Could Wizard Aduro have been wrong? Or was Sepron so far away that he couldn't feel the summons?

As they sailed further out to sea, Elenna leant over the side. "I can see something moving!" she cried.

Tom's stomach lurched. *Sepron?* he asked himself. *Or Zepha?*

Joy flooded through him as a huge head and arching neck burst out of the sea, glittering streams of water pouring from it. Tom gazed up at Sepron's shining eyes and rainbow-coloured scales.

"It worked!" Elenna laughed.

The great sea serpent arched his
neck protectively over the boat. Then
he dived beneath the waves again.
Even though Tom couldn't see him,
he knew that the Beast was there,
ready to help and protect them.
Would it be enough? Or was Malvel's
evil Beast too strong even for Sepron?

By now Tom could see the turbulent
water at the edge of the whirlpool.
Silver began to whine and pace back

and forth along the boards of the boat.

"He knows something's wrong," Elenna said grimly.

Gripping his shield, Tom climbed onto the boat's side, Elenna scrambling up beside him.

"I'll distract Zepha," Tom said. "When he comes after me, you grab the helmet and swim back to the boat as fast as you can."

Elenna nodded.

Tom gazed down into the whirlpool. Just below the surface Sepron was circling, waiting.

"Stay, Silver," Elenna told the wolf. He whimpered a little, but settled down obediently in the bottom of the boat with his nose on his paws.

"This is it," Tom said.

Together, he and Elenna dived into the whirlpool.

CHAPTER NINE

THE ANGER OF ZEPHA

This time the weight of Tom's sword and shield took him down faster. He managed to keep his sense of direction, swimming in a spiral down to the sea bed. He looked up. Above him, Elenna swam with Sepron.

Soon Tom spotted the coral reef and the golden glint of the helmet. He pointed Elenna towards it. Elenna

put her thumbs up and began to
head in that direction.

Then the huge form of Zepha came
into view behind the spires of coral.
Tom saw Elenna's mouth open in
a cry of horror. Valuable air bubbled
away to the surface. Tom had to help!
He swam close to her and gripped her
shoulder encouragingly.

Then they swam on together
towards the menacing shape of the
monster squid.

As they drew closer, Tom could
see the giant tentacles waving gently
in the underwater tide. Zepha was
curled up as if he were resting. But
Tom wasn't fooled.

In a sudden movement, Elenna
darted towards the helmet. Tom
swam nearer, despite the danger,
hoping to distract the evil Beast.
But he got too close. As Tom

turned to swim away, hoping Zepha would be lured to follow, a tentacle lashed out and wrapped itself round his ankle.

Tom tugged furiously, trying to free himself. He spotted Elenna swimming towards him, but waved her back, towards the helmet.

He could feel the tentacle tightening. It was cutting off his blood supply; his foot was growing numb. He kicked out, trying to swim for the surface, but the tentacle held him back. Starting to panic, Tom gulped in a mouthful of sea water and began to choke. Then he caught another glimpse of Elenna. Her knife in her hand, she was swimming down towards the giant squid. She pulled her arm back, and the knife flashed in a shaft of sunlight that pierced the sea-green gloom. Then she thrust the blade

deep into the tough muscle of
Zepha's tentacle.

The Beast's pale eyes opened wide
in a spasm of pain and fury. Tom felt
the grip on his ankle loosen. Drawing
his sword, he slashed angrily at the
tentacle. Red blood billowed out into
the water. The tip of the tentacle fell
away as the Beast thrashed wildly in

agony. Tom was free – for the moment.

He swam away from Zepha, but the squid heaved his injured body up from the coral bed and gave chase, closing the gap between himself and Tom with frightening speed.

Then Tom saw Sepron swimming towards them. His scales glittered and his eyes flashed with fury.

The sea serpent's jaws gaped as he snapped angrily at Zepha. His teeth punctured the squid's leathery skin and gripped tightly.

Zepha twisted with rage and pain, and squirted a huge cloud of black ink from the underside of his body into the sea serpent's face. Sepron reared back, blinded by the ink, and thrashed his head from side to side as the black cloud spread. His grip on Zepha loosened as he rolled over and over in the water, trying to clear his sight.

Free again, the monster squid shot after Tom. His tentacles whipped through the sea, churning up underwater currents. Tom was battered around by the angry water. Where was Elenna? He couldn't see her! He swiped at Zepha with his sword, aiming at the three hearts that pulsed beneath the squid's skin.

But one flailing tentacle knocked
the sword out of his hand. Tom stared
in horror as it sank and was lost in the
darkness of the green, watery depths.

Tom had never felt so alone. Sepron couldn't help him, and Elenna had vanished. His arms and legs ached with exhaustion, and the air in his lungs was running out again. He struck out for the surface, but he knew he would never swim fast enough to escape, and he had no weapon left with which to fight.

Zepha swam towards Tom, his mouth open wide. His pale eyes gleamed. One of his tentacles coiled round Tom's waist. Terrified, Tom felt himself being dragged closer to that gaping hole. He held up his shield as a last attempt to defend himself. But Zepha's mouth was big enough to engulf the shield and Tom as well.

Malvel had won. There was nothing more Tom could do.

CHAPTER TEN

VICTORY?

Suddenly the water swirled as
Elenna swam in front of Tom, his
sword gripped in one hand, her knife
in the other. Fearlessly she plunged
down and forced the sword into
Zepha's open mouth, jamming the
beak open. The squid's bulging eyes
flared with anger. He released
his grip on Tom and flung all his
tentacles at Elenna. More bubbles

escaped from her mouth as she
gasped in alarm. She turned and
swam rapidly away.

Tom knew he hadn't much time.
The sword wouldn't keep Zepha back
for long and he couldn't hold his
breath for much longer. He had to
find the helmet, but in the battle
with the squid he had lost his sense
of direction. He peered down
through the gloom, but he couldn't
see the tell-tale glint of gold.

To his relief, Sepron came gliding
through the greenish darkness. Tom
could tell he had recovered his sight;
his eyes glared with anger and he
was heading straight for Zepha.
He swooped down and wrapped his
rainbow-coloured coils around the
squid. He twisted to and fro so that
Zepha couldn't squirt ink into his face
again, or grip him with his tentacles.

Sepron clutched the giant squid
tighter and tighter with his coils. Tom

could hardly believe what he was seeing. It looked as if the sea serpent was squeezing the life out of Zepha. Astonished, Tom watched as the edges of Zepha started to blur. He looked round for Elenna, who had reappeared, and pointed frantically. Something was happening! Rippling movements came from beneath Zepha's skin as the evil Beast writhed in agony.

Suddenly the monster squid's three pulsing, red hearts shattered into tiny glinting pieces, too many for Tom to count, and his skin burst open, tearing cruelly. Tom struggled not to gasp underwater as thousands of tiny squid shot out, swimming as if they feared for their lives. Zepha's empty, papery skin began to sink slowly down into the gloom, towards the sea bed. He was no more.

Elenna grabbed Tom's sword before it could fall out of sight once again. Tom swam after her, gazing round for a glimpse of the helmet. Then he spotted its golden gleam.

But exhaustion made his limbs heavy. He had no air left. His lungs were screaming with pain. Elenna must be feeling the same. Were they going to die after all?

Then Tom caught sight of Sepron swimming towards them. The sea serpent dived underneath them and rose slowly upwards so that Tom and Elenna could cling to his scaly neck as he headed for the surface. Tom hugged Sepron with relief.

As they passed the coral spire where the golden helmet rested, Tom reached out and grasped it by the hooked beak.

Sepron's neck rose out of the water just beside the boat. Tom and

Elenna clung on for a moment more, gasping air into their tortured lungs. Silver sprang up and rested his front paws on the side of the boat, letting out an astonished yelp.

Then the sea serpent lowered his neck. Tom and Elenna gently rolled off into the bottom of the boat. Silver pushed up close to Elenna, nosing her. She rolled onto her back and allowed the wolf to lick her face. Her chest rose and fell as she gasped for air. Then she reached out a hand to ruffle Silver's fur. She was all right.

"Thank you, Sepron," Tom panted, reaching up to pat the serpent's gleaming scales. "We couldn't have done it without you."

Sepron bowed his head and gave each of them a friendly touch with his nose before sinking back beneath the waves again. Tom caught a last glimpse of his rainbow coils as he swam away into the open sea. He felt warmed by the thought that the Beast who had once been his foe had saved their lives.

"Well," he said with an exhausted sigh. "We've got the helmet."

"Why don't you try it on?" Elenna asked, climbing to her feet.

Tom hesitated for a moment, turning the helmet over between his hands. The gold shone brightly and he could see how skilfully the helmet was crafted from the time he had spent working in his uncle's forge.

Could it really be for him? Was he worthy of wearing the helmet that once belonged to the Master of the Beasts of Avantia?

"Go on!" Elenna urged him.

Tom raised the helmet and put it on his head. Instantly he felt it shrink to fit him. He gasped. His eyesight had suddenly grown stronger! He could see the people on the shoreline; Calum's father was mending a fishing net and Lindon was squatting by the fire, drinking something from a bowl. Further away from the sea, Calum was leading Storm along the edge of the trees. Tom could even see the whites of the stallion's eyes as he paced up and down.

"This is amazing," he exclaimed.

"I can see everything! I just wish my father, Taladon, could see me."

"He'd be so proud of you," Elenna told him.

Tom and Elenna hugged each other. Triumph bubbled up inside Tom. The first part of his new Quest was over! He had retrieved the helmet. And now he was determined that it wouldn't be long before he found the other five parts of the armour, too.

"We've only just started," he said to Elenna. "I'm not giving up until I have every piece of the golden armour."

Elenna smiled in agreement. "Let's get back to shore," she said gently.

She pulled up the sail and began to guide the boat towards the beach.

They were halfway back when a familiar blue glow began to appear before them, and Aduro seemed to stand on the waves.

But this time he was not alone.

Standing behind him was Malvel, who held a slim, jewelled dagger to the wizard's neck. Aduro's face was set hard, as if he was refusing to show fear.

Tom couldn't understand what he was seeing. "Get away from him!" he shouted at Malvel.

The Dark Wizard smiled. "So you have the golden helmet," he sneered.

"But I don't suppose you feel quite so pleased with yourself now, do you?"

"I don't believe this!" Tom cried. "It's just an illusion. You could never take Aduro prisoner. You haven't the power."

"I'm afraid I do." Malvel dug the point of the dagger into Aduro's neck. "Tell them, fool."

"This is a true vision," Wizard Aduro said reluctantly. "Perhaps I was foolish, and didn't guard myself well enough. I am Malvel's prisoner."

"I'll free you!" Tom said defiantly.

Malvel's cruel laughter sounded. "You can try."

Tom reached out to Aduro, but his hand passed through air. "Tell me what to do!"

"You can free me," Wizard Aduro said. "But first you must find the full suit of armour… It is the only way."

"That will never happen," Malvel interrupted, the dagger digging into the good wizard's neck. "You'll fail the next test, Tom, when you have to face my second evil Beast – Claw."

"We'll do it," Tom vowed. "We'll free Aduro and destroy you once and for all."

"I can hold out against him," Aduro insisted, though his face was pale. "But you must complete the Quest!"

Malvel's laughter rang out again as the vision faded.

Tom and Elenna exchanged a horrified glance. All Tom's sense of triumph had vanished. He could only think about Aduro in the clutches of Malvel.

As they beached the boat, Calum came up to them, leading Storm. Tom had been wondering how to explain to Lindon why they had taken his boat without permission, but thankfully, the fisherman was nowhere in sight. Tom climbed out of the boat and took the stallion's reins, stroking his nose.

"Thanks," he said to Calum. Glancing out to sea again, he added, "I don't think you'll have any more trouble."

Calum met his gaze steadily. "I won't ask questions," he said. "You saved us once before, and that's good enough for me." He bent to give Silver a pat. "You're welcome to come and stay with my family if you want."

"Thank you, but we can't," Tom said regretfully. "We have other duties."

"I understand," said Calum. "But I hope you'll come back when you can. You'll always find friends here."

Taking up his sword and shield, Tom climbed into Storm's saddle with Elenna behind him.

"Farewell!" Elenna called.

"Farewell, and good luck!" Calum replied.

With a last wave, Tom and Elenna headed up the beach to find the road that led back inland.

Tom felt as if a huge weight was pressing upon him. "This is our most important Quest yet," he said.

"I know." Elenna tightened her arms around his waist. "This time we've got to succeed."

Tom nodded. She was right. The Quest wasn't about his need to prove himself, not any more. It wasn't even about the magical golden armour.

It was about rescuing Aduro.

Could they do it?

"While there's blood in my veins," Tom swore, "I'll never give up!"

Join Tom on the next stage
of the Beast Quest

Meet

CLAW
THE
GIANT MONKEY

Can Tom and Elenna collect the
golden armour and free Avantia?

PROLOGUE

The air was hot and humid. The market trader mopped his brow and stared into the thick mass of jungle trees before him. They reminded him of rotten black teeth. Heavy vines hung down like snakes.

"Do we have to go there?" asked the boy at the trader's side. "Is there no other way?"

"We've travelled hundreds of miles for the Ruby Guya fruit," the trader reminded his assistant. "It grows nowhere else in Avantia. Only here in the Dark Jungle."

"But aren't there monsters who live here? That's what people say," the boy whispered.

Everyone in Avantia knew the terrors of the Dark Jungle: creatures that plucked men from the ground and ate them whole; plants whose rich scents could overwhelm a person at twenty paces. Few dared to enter – and fewer still returned.

"Rumours to frighten honest men," said the trader with a wave of his hand.

"Is it true the Ruby Guya possesses miraculous powers?" the boy asked.

The trader nodded. "One bite of its sweet red flesh brings courage to the faint-hearted and strength to the weak," he said. "It is only ever seen at the king's table, and fetches a price beyond rubies." He glanced at his young assistant. "But we must keep our heads if we are to harvest it. Do you understand?"

The boy swallowed his fear and nodded.

They entered the jungle side by side. At once the light grew dim. The ground was marshy beneath their feet and there was a stench of rotting vegetation. Birds screamed and wheeled overhead. Great tree ferns arched above them, their leaves a bright and poisonous green.

The trader gazed at the fleshy jungle flowers that hung in ropes from the trees. They smelled over-ripe and dangerous. He forced all thoughts of creatures and deadly scents from his mind. But he couldn't shake the feeling that something was watching them.

A branch crashed to the ground. The trader whirled, pulling his knife from its sheath in one swift movement. But all he saw were shadows.

They walked on. Soon they found themselves wading through a foul-smelling swamp. The thick, pungent water lapped at their knees. The trader clenched his teeth to stop them from trembling. Who knew what vile creatures lurked at his feet?

He wanted to weep with relief when they touched solid ground again.

"We must press on," he said.

The boy crawled out of the swamp. "Leeches," he sobbed. "They're all over me!"

The trader prised the leeches from the boy's bare ankles with the blade of his knife. With a shudder, he did the same to the bloodsuckers on his own legs. The Dark Jungle was a terrible, stinking place. He would be glad to leave – once he had found the fruit he sought.

They moved on. Splashes of sunlight seemed to drip to the ground like venom. Monkeys chattered in the highest treetops above them. It sounded as if they were laughing.

At last, through the ferns, the trader glimpsed a cluster of trees with green, waxy leaves and plump red fruits. His heart leapt.

The Ruby Guya!

The trader hauled himself into the nearest tree, laughing with delight.

"Come on, boy!" he called behind him. "This fruit is ripe for the picking. Where are you?"

He looked back over his shoulder. The boy had disappeared. Uneasy now, the trader glanced around the clearing. Something was not right.

There was a scuffling sound in the undergrowth – and then a terrible scream. The trader froze.

Suddenly a gnarled claw shot out of the foliage and grabbed the fruit from the trader's hand. The man screamed as a hairy face with bloodshot eyes emerged from behind the green leaves. Huge lips curled back to reveal thick, yellow teeth.

"Boy!" the trader croaked. "Run!"

Then his eyes darted to the jungle floor and what he saw made his blood run cold. All that remained of his companion were strips of torn linen from the boy's tunic.

Slowly, the trader looked back at the Beast. It was too late for escape. He howled as a long, thick tail with a deadly claw on its tip flicked out and wrapped itself round his waist.

The trader's screams echoed around the jungle clearing. Then he was gone.

CHAPTER ONE

CROSSING THE WINDING RIVER

Tom guided his black stallion, Storm, inland, away from Avantia's western shore. Elenna sat quietly behind him, her arms around his waist. Silver, Elenna's pet wolf, padded quietly alongside. Struggling with Zepha the monster squid had been their toughest challenge yet. If it hadn't been for Sepron, the great sea serpent and protector of Avantia's waters, they might never have defeated the evil Beast.

In Storm's saddlebag lay a magnificent golden helmet, shaped like the head of an eagle. It was the first piece from the great suit of golden armour, which gave magical powers to its rightful owner. The armour had belonged to the Master of the Beasts and had been destined to pass to Tom as a reward for completing his first Quest. Now it was Tom's fate to recover the six pieces, which had been stolen by the Dark Wizard, Malvel, and scattered across Avantia. But Malvel had created six evil Beasts to protect each piece. Zepha had been the first, with the helmet as the prize. There were five more Beasts to overcome and five pieces of armour to collect.

But that was not all. For Malvel had taken more than the armour. He had kidnapped Aduro, King Hugo's wizard and Tom and Elenna's friend and protector.

"I'm worried about Aduro," Elenna said now.

"That's why we have to find and defeat this next Beast, Claw, whatever he is," said Tom. "We will soon find all six pieces of the armour and, when our Quest is complete, we will rescue Aduro. As he told us himself, there's no other way!"

Silver yapped in excitement, and Storm tossed his fine head.

"Malvel may have Aduro," said Tom, "but we still have Aduro's enchanted map. Let's see if it will tell us where we can find Claw."

They dismounted and Tom drew the parchment scroll from the saddlebag. As he unrolled it, the map sprang to life. The mountains of Avantia rose as high as his thumb

and tiny waves crashed onto the map's shores.
Tom and Elenna shared a smile. No matter
how many times they used the magical map,
it never failed to amaze them.

Slowly the image on the map began to slide
down, revealing new terrain in the south. The
landscape grew greener. Suddenly a glowing
red line appeared from Avantia's western shore
and snaked down, past the Winding River, into
a small patch of green in the southeast.

Elenna put her finger to the spot, then
started and pulled her hand away in surprise.
Her finger was warm and damp.

"I have an idea where we might be headed,"
said Tom, frowning. "There's a place called the
Dark Jungle in the southeast. The people of
Avantia rarely go there."

"Why not?" Elenna asked.

"The Dark Jungle is hot and dangerous," Tom
told her. "Strange creatures live in it. There are
poisonous plants and spiders the size of your
fist. I've heard that if the heat and the insects
don't kill you, the creatures will."

Elenna shuddered.

Tom studied the map more closely. Something
was moving in the depths of the Dark Jungle.

It glimmered, then disappeared again.

"Look," Tom said, showing Elenna the map. "Can you see? That tiny gold dot. Look closely."

"It's the chainmail!" Elenna said excitedly. "The next piece of the armour!"

Tom rolled up the map. "We're going to the Dark Jungle," he said. "There's no time to lose!"

Follow this Quest to the end in CLAW THE GIANT MONKEY.

Fight the Beasts,
Fear the Magic

www.beastquest.co.uk

Have you checked out the all-new Beast Quest website?
It's the place to go for games, downloads, activities,
sneak previews and lots of fun!

You can read all about your favourite Beast Quest
monsters, download free screensavers and desktop
wallpapers for your computer, and send
beastly e-cards to your friends.

Sign up to the newsletter at www.beastquest.co.uk
to receive exclusive extra content and the opportunity
to enter special members-only competitions. It's the best
place to go for up-to-date info on all the Beast Quest
books, including the next exciting series,
which features six brand new Beasts.

Win an exclusive
Beast Quest T-shirt and goody bag!

In every Beast Quest book the Beast Quest logo
is hidden in one of the pictures. Find the logos in
book 7 to book 12 and make a note of which pages
they appear on. Send the six page numbers in to us.
Each month we will draw one winner to receive
a Beast Quest T-shirt and goody bag.

Send your entry on a postcard listing the titles
of books 7–12, the winning page numbers in each
book and your name, age and address to:

BEAST QUEST: THE GOLDEN ARMOUR COMPETITION
Orchard Books
338 Euston Road
London NW1 3BH

Australian readers should write to:

Orchard Books Australia
Level 17/207 Kent Street
Sydney, NSW 2000

Only one entry per child.
Final draw: 30 May 2009

You can also enter this competition
via the Beast Quest website: www.beastquest.co.uk

by Adam Blade

Series 1

Series 2: The Golden Armour

All priced at £4.99
Vedra & Krimon: Twin Beasts of Avantia is priced at £5.99

The Beast Quest books are available from all good
bookshops, or can be ordered direct from the publisher:
Orchard Books, PO BOX 29, Douglas IM99 1BQ.
Credit card orders please telephone 01624 836000
or fax 01624 837033 or visit our website: www.orchardbooks.co.uk
or e-mail: bookshop@enterprise.net for details.

To order please quote title, author
and ISBN and your full name and address.
Cheques and postal orders should be made payable to 'Bookpost plc.'
Postage and packing is FREE within the UK
(overseas customers should add £2.00 per book).

Prices and availability are subject to change.